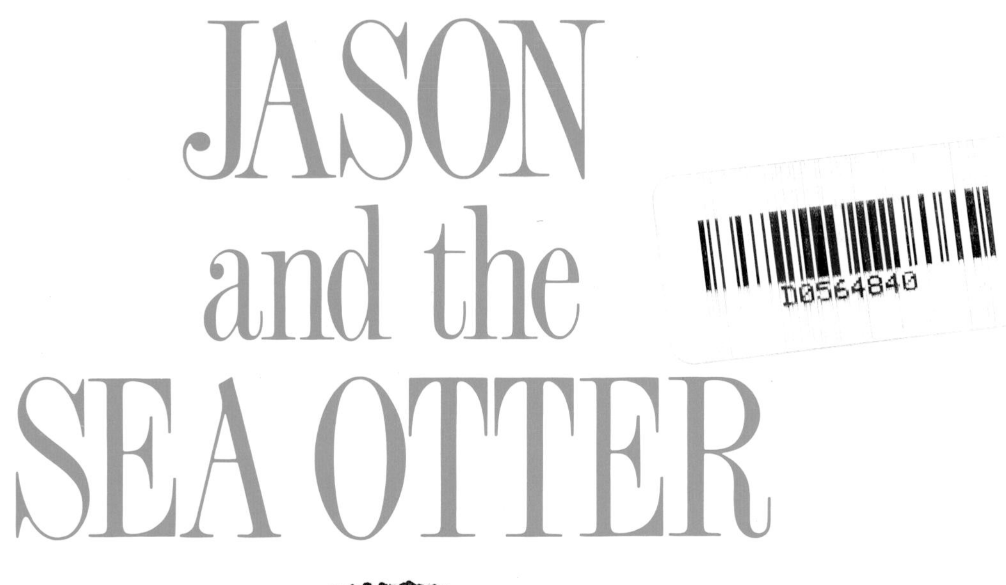

JASON and the SEA OTTER

By Joe Barber-Starkey

Illustrated by Paul Montpellier

Fourth paperback printing, 2004.

Harbour Publishing
P.O. Box 219
Madeira Park, BC Canada VON 2H0
Website: www.harbourpublishing.com

Design by Roger Handling Terra Firma Design

Canadian Cataloguing in Publication Data

Barber-Starkey, Joe, 1918-
Jason and the sea otter

ISBN 0-920080-31-6 (bound) – ISBN 1-55017-162-3 (pbk)

I. Montpellier, Paul 1949- II. Title.
PS8553.A743J3 1989 JC813'.54 C87-091390-5
PZ7.B37Ja 1989

Printed in China through Colorcraft Ltd. Hong Kong

The summer sun was warm on Jason's brown back as he leaned over the side of his canoe and jigged his cod-fishing line up and down from the sea bottom. The canoe was tied to a kelp bed, a shiny brown tangle of giant seaweed outside the gap between the two islands which protected his home village from the wild winds and pounding waves of winter storms.

The weather had been calm for many days now, and the long swell of the ocean rocked the canoe gently. The smell of the cedar of the dugout canoe and of the tar which patched its ancient hull combined with the background odours of salt water and seaweed, while an occasional offshore movement of air brought the delicious scent of the sunbaked needles which were thick on the ground under the spruce trees on the islands. The soft cries of the drowsy sea birds, the soothing sounds of humming insects and the gentle lapping sound of the water against the canoe did not make him want to do anything else but to be still, watch and listen.

It was a lazy day, and after catching a fat codfish Jason lost interest in fishing and picked up the old bottomless plastic pail which he had found on a beach. He held it down over the side of the canoe so that he could use it as a window to look down under the water. The reflection of the light from the sky and the shadow of his head made it difficult to see anything at first, but he found that by pulling his jacket over his head, like an old-fashioned photographer, the underwater world suddenly became clear.

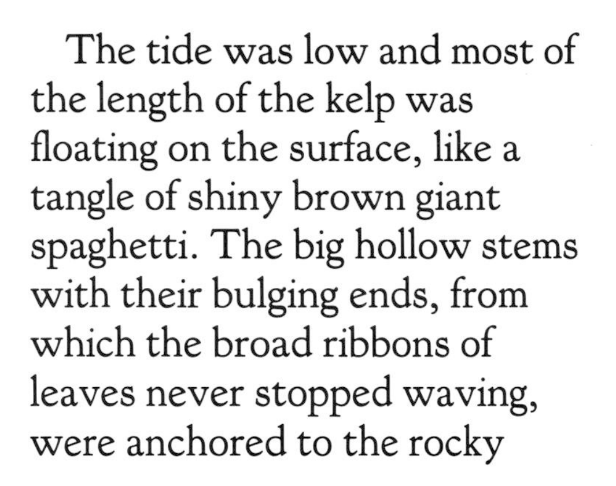

The tide was low and most of the length of the kelp was floating on the surface, like a tangle of shiny brown giant spaghetti. The big hollow stems with their bulging ends, from which the broad ribbons of leaves never stopped waving, were anchored to the rocky bottom of the sea by long slender stalks, which were so strong that the Indians had used them for canoe anchor ropes before the white man came. They had also found a use for the fat bulbs of the kelp heads as bottles for storing fish oil and medicines.

As Jason gazed down through the forest of kelp stems he could see the richness of the life in the water—the little kelp crabs, snails and spider crabs on the stems, and the clouds of tiny living particles that were food for the schools of baby herring which moved together as if controlled by one brain, flashing in the light as they

turned suddenly to avoid a hungry fish. The water was so clear that Jason could see right to the rocky sea bottom with its rich life of shellfish, crabs, and sea urchins, and the colourful plumes of sea pens and anemones, all enjoying the abundance of food which was carried in by the waves and strong tides.

The dugout canoe, which was anchored by its rope to one of the kelp stems, looked very like an old log of driftwood, and the boy was so still under his covering jacket that no bird or animal would have guessed that he was there. Not that Jason would have frightened any of his wild friends on purpose, because he loved them all and he had found out how to come close to them by moving slowly and quietly, sometimes talking to them softly, using the words he had learned from his old grandfather.

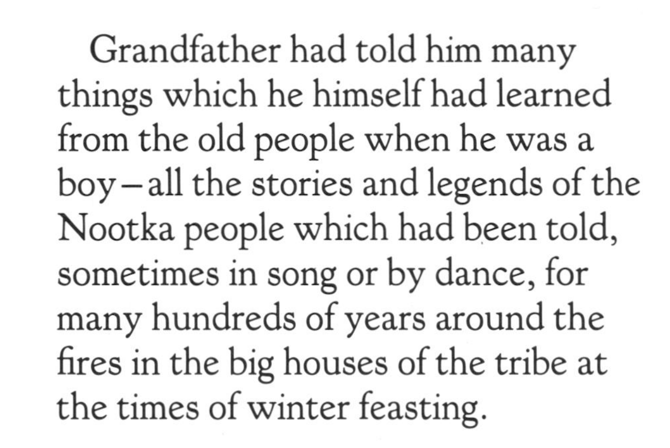

Grandfather had told him many things which he himself had learned from the old people when he was a boy – all the stories and legends of the Nootka people which had been told, sometimes in song or by dance, for many hundreds of years around the fires in the big houses of the tribe at the times of winter feasting.

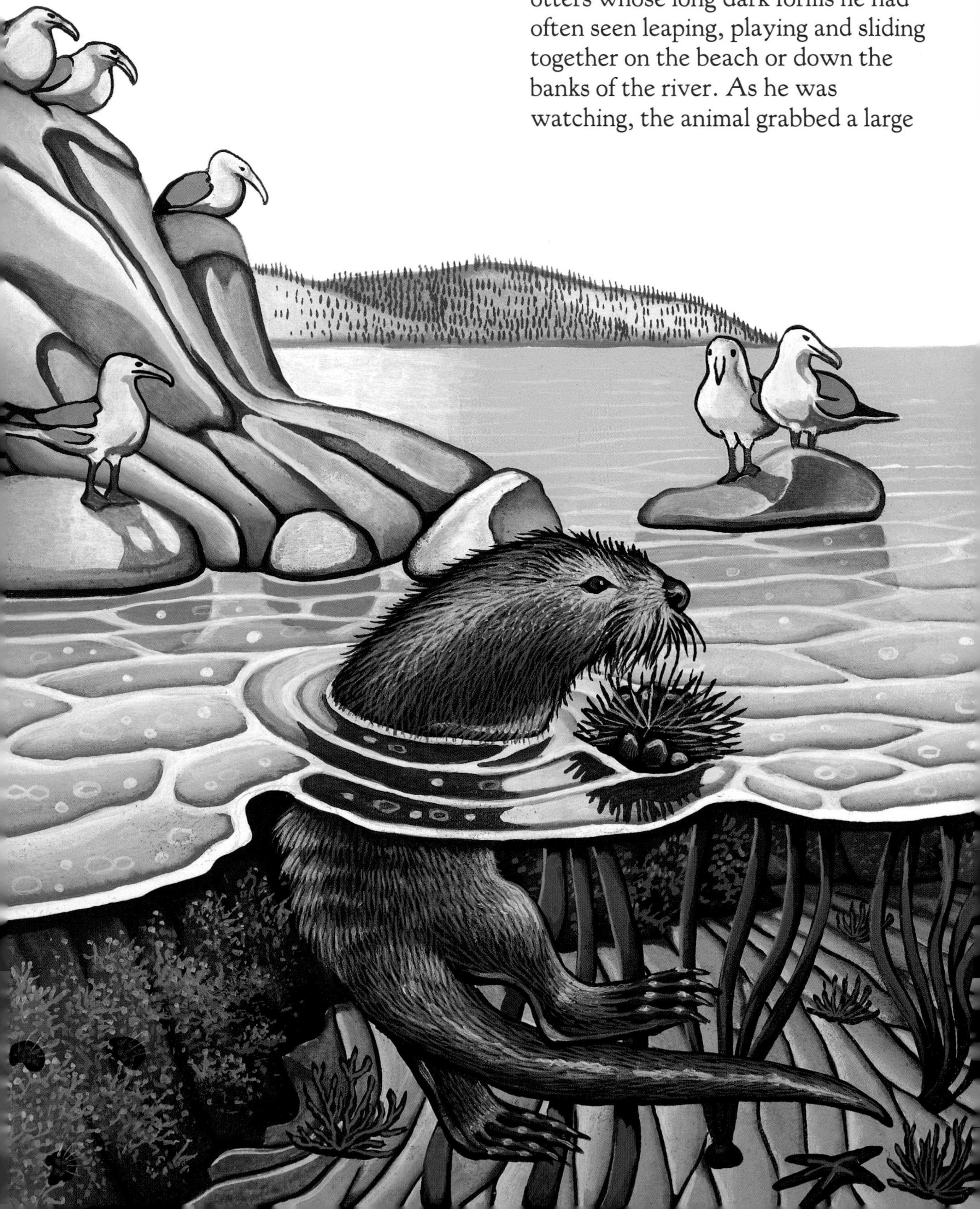

Suddenly Jason's eyes opened wide as he saw something dark swimming like a big fish among the kelp stems near the bottom. He couldn't think what it could be, as it was much bigger than a mink, but too small and the wrong shape and colour for a seal. He thought it might be one of the river otters whose long dark forms he had often seen leaping, playing and sliding together on the beach or down the banks of the river. As he was watching, the animal grabbed a large spiny sea urchin from the bottom with its front paw and swam toward the surface.

Jason slowly raised his head from the pail, keeping under the cover of his jacket, and looked to see where the animal would come up. The bright reflection of the sun on the shining kelp made it hard to see, but suddenly he saw a dark furry head with black eyes and a grey whiskery muzzle bobbing among the weeds, looking like a friendly little old man. As Jason watched, the animal twisted a leg around some kelp, then lay on its back and started to eat the sea urchin, not seeming to care about having a mouthful of prickles.

For over an hour Jason watched in fascination as the animal took turns to dive for food and then to lie on the surface to eat it. After the meal the animal started to groom itself all over very carefully, using its front paws like a comb to arrange its outer waterproof coat and blowing in air to fluff up the soft inner fur which insulated its body from the cold of the water.

Jason had been swimming already this summer at the mouth of the river by his home village. There the rising tide came up over the mudflats that had baked all day in the sun, making the water warm, but he knew better than to try swimming in the cold sea outside the islands, with its treacherous currents and tide-rips that could pull even a big log under the surface.

The animal went to sleep in the sun, lying on its back with a strand of kelp twisted around one leg, so Jason quietly loosened his canoe rope and paddled swiftly through the harbour entrance to his village. He couldn't wait to tell his grandfather about what he had seen.

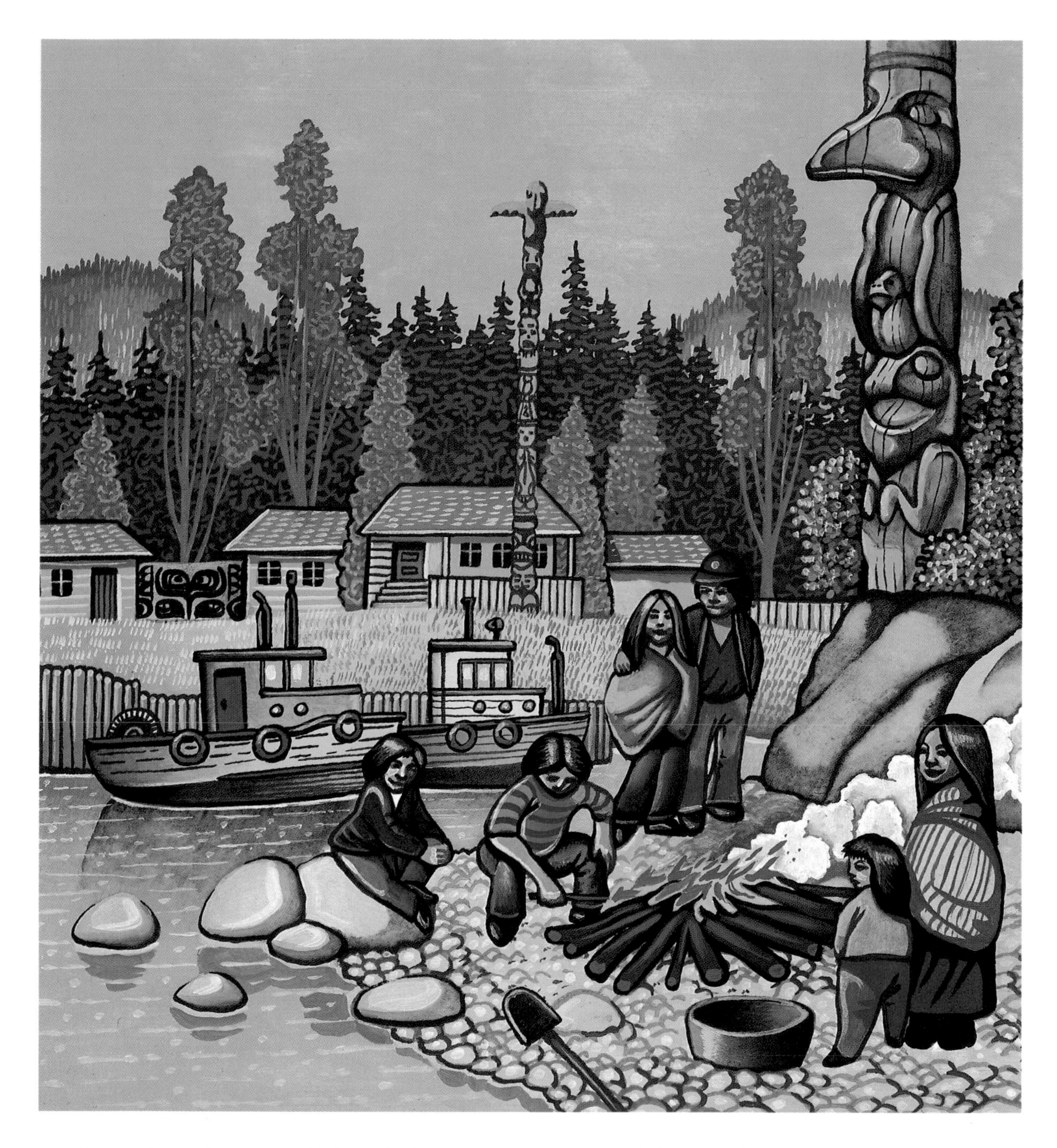

The village houses all faced the sea at the top of a high, curving gravel beach, where great mounds of broken white clamshells told the story of many delicious feasts of clams baked in pits of steaming seaweed under blazing fires of driftwood.

Jason, his mother and grandfather, were the only people living in the winter village at this time, looking after it while all the rest of their Nootka band were busy at the summer village catching their winter food supply of salmon and preserving it by smoking or drying it in the sun.

Grandfather was sitting in his favourite chair in the evening sun, and as soon as Jason had cleaned the fish and given it to his mother to cook, he hurried to where the old man was dreaming of days gone by. Grandfather did not like to be hurried at any time, and after Jason had gabbled out the story of what he had seen, the old man closed his eyes for a few moments before he gave his reply in the slow and gentle voice of his people.

"Yes, Jason, what you have seen is the Sea Otter. My father's father told the story of how, when he was a boy, there were very many of these animals in nearly every kelp bed all up and down this coast. Then the white men came in their big sailing ships, with stories that the fur of the sea otter was worth much money in the lands across the ocean, so they hunted and killed the animals until, after a very few years, there were none to be found in this part of the coast. They were hunted not only by the white men with their guns and harpoons, but some of our own people were greedy too, and killed the animals with which they had lived in peace for so many hundreds of years. But now at last one has come back—we must tell no one of our secret, or they could be in danger again."

After that day Jason spent many hours with his canoe tied to the kelp bed, watching the sea otter. He never tired of seeing how clever it was at getting its food of sea urchins, starfish, crabs, abalone and other shellfish from the sea bottom, and at its funny habit of lying back like a whiskered old man while using its chest for a dining table. On one occasion he saw the otter tuck a large clam into the loose fold of skin under its chin and then pick up a flat stone from the bottom of the sea before swimming to the surface. Once there, it lay on its back with the stone flat on its chest, and pounded the clam on it until the shell broke and the inside could be eaten. "Not so dumb," whispered Jason to himself.

The animal was not afraid of Jason if he was careful to move slowly and did not stand up in the canoe or make a noise. But he did disturb things on the day that he found out that there were two otters!

He was watching through his pail, leaning over the side of the canoe as usual, when the first otter was suddenly joined by another one, and their underwater games and acrobatics so interested and amused Jason that he forgot to be careful, and leaned over too far. A sudden gust of wind caught the canoe and tipped it sideways, throwing Jason head first into the sea. The icy water made him gasp, and he swallowed some, which made him choke, before he could struggle clear of the jacket which had

been over his head. He was halfway to the bottom, with his ears ringing and his chest hurting, before he remembered that he could swim and pushed his way upwards, fighting through the tangled stems of the kelp. At last he got his head above water, coughing and spluttering, and was glad to have the kelp to hang onto while he caught his breath, but his heart sank when he looked around and saw that the canoe had come loose from where he had tied it and was moving slowly away from him.

Jason felt very worried and frightened, for it was not possible for him to swim through the tangled kelp, over the slippery surface of which the canoe was sliding so easily with the powerful tide. He remembered that his father and other fishermen had said that a person who fell into the ocean could not live for more than a few minutes before being overcome by the cold water.

Suddenly the canoe stopped moving, although the current seemed to be as strong as ever. Jason knew that he had to get to it quickly, but that his only choice was to swim around the outside of the kelp bed to where the canoe seemed to be caught. He started off, swimming as hard as he could, fearful that at any minute the canoe might free itself again and leave him stranded, with no hope of ever reaching the shore because of the powerful tide.

After what seemed to him to be hours of struggle, with the cold water numbing his arms and legs until they ached, he reached the canoe at last. After three tries he managed to pull himself into it, crawling carefully over the stern so as not to tip it. All the time he had been swimming he was telling himself off for being so clumsy and not fastening the rope more carefully. There was some water in the bottom of the canoe, but not enough to stop it being used safely, and luckily his paddle was caught under one of the extra crosspieces that had been used to repair the old dugout.

Because of his own danger he had forgotten all about the sea otters, and when he looked for the end of his anchor rope to free it, he could hardly believe his eyes. One of the otters was lying on the surface among the kelp, contentedly munching on a crab, with one of its legs holding a kelp stem while the other was twisted around the canoe rope. So that was what had stopped the drifting canoe! Jason talked quietly to the otter while he pulled gently on the rope to free it, thanking it for saving his life by stopping the canoe.

He lifted his paddle to start for home, still shivering with fright and cold, but as he turned to take a last look at his otter friend he was quite sure that it closed one eye and winked at him. As he headed home through the harbour entrance he was thinking of what an exciting story he would have to tell to his grandchildren when he was a grandfather.